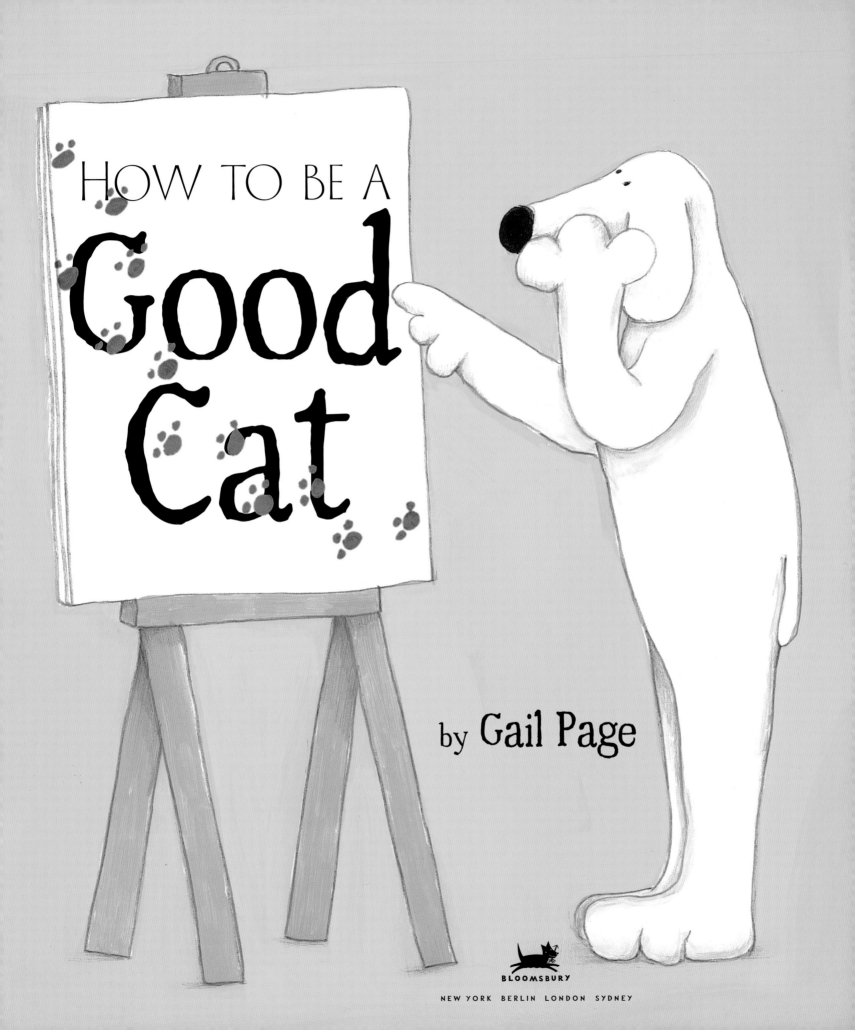

How to be a Good Cat

by Gail Page

BLOOMSBURY

NEW YORK BERLIN LONDON SYDNEY

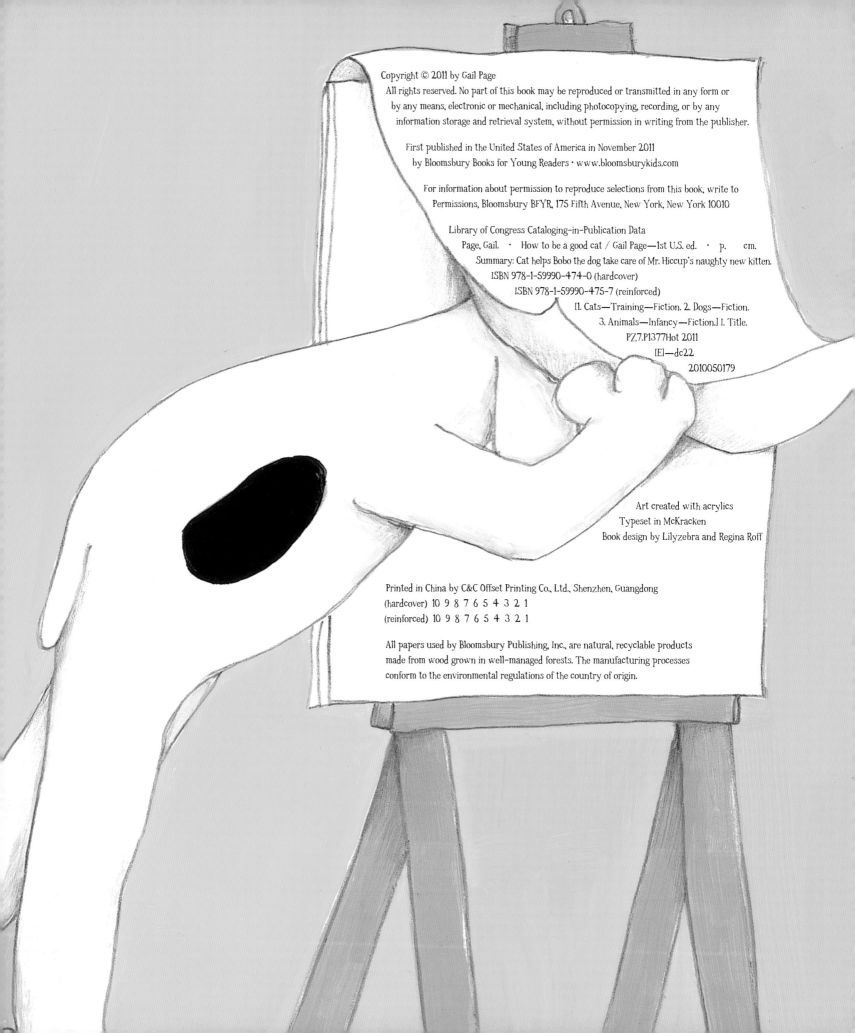

First published in the United States of America in November 2011
by Bloomsbury Books for Young Readers · www.bloomsburykids.com

For information about permission to reproduce selections from this book, write to
Permissions, Bloomsbury BFYR, 175 Fifth Avenue, New York, New York 10010

Library of Congress Cataloging-in-Publication Data
Page, Gail.   ·   How to be a good cat / Gail Page—1st U.S. ed.   ·   p.   cm.
Summary: Cat helps Bobo the dog take care of Mr. Hiccup's naughty new kitten.
ISBN 978-1-59990-474-0 (hardcover)
ISBN 978-1-59990-475-7 (reinforced)
[1. Cats—Training—Fiction. 2. Dogs—Fiction.
3. Animals—Infancy—Fiction.] I. Title.
PZ7.P1377Hot 2011
[E]—dc22
2010050179

Art created with acrylics
Typeset in McKracken
Book design by Lilyzebra and Regina Roff

Printed in China by C&C Offset Printing Co., Ltd., Shenzhen, Guangdong
(hardcover) 10 9 8 7 6 5 4 3 2 1
(reinforced) 10 9 8 7 6 5 4 3 2 1

All papers used by Bloomsbury Publishing, Inc., are natural, recyclable products
made from wood grown in well-managed forests. The manufacturing processes
conform to the environmental regulations of the country of origin.

Dedicated to Robert Shetterly

Bobo was good.
He liked to help.

So when Mr. Hiccup asked Mrs. Birdhead
if someone could look after his kitten,

Bobo volunteered!

Bonkers wasn't just **very cute,**

he was also very . . .

GHTY!

Bobo tried all the tricks he knew.

Sit was **difficult.**

Fetch was **worse.**

Stay was a **complete disaster.**

Nothing worked.

How could Bobo teach Bonkers to be a good cat?

Luckily, he knew **just** who to call.

Lesson #1:
Cats are **sneaky.**
You never see them coming.

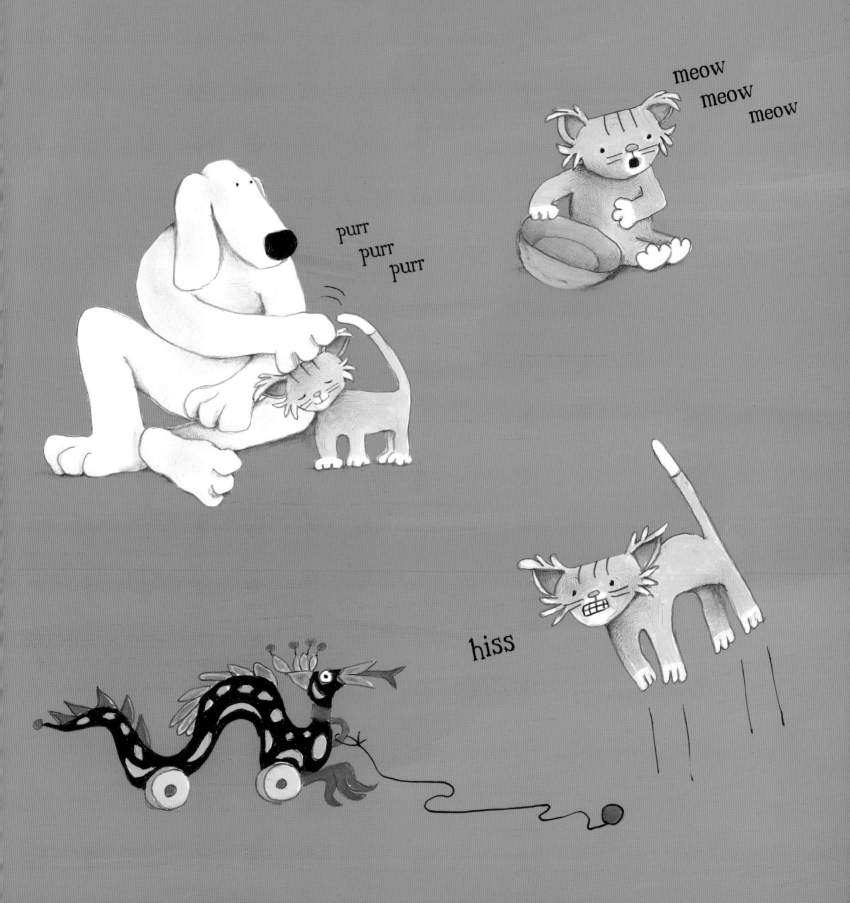

Lesson #3:
Cats are stretchy.

It helps them balance and **pounce!**

Lesson #4:
Cats are very clean.

But they **don't** like water.

Lesson #5:
Cats like to **climb.**

And **they** always land on their feet.

In no time at all, the lessons were done.
Now Bobo knew all about cats.

Cats Sneak.

bark bark bark

Cats Chat.

meow meow meow

Cats Stretch.

Cats are Clean.

Cats Climb.

But **Bobo** taught Bonkers something too . . .

How to take a **cat** nap.

The end.